Wandering Through Unlikely Worlds

Dhruva Chak

Tara Press

Wandering Through Unlikely Worlds
Dhruva Chak

Tara Press
Flat No. 6, Khan Market, New Delhi - 110 003
Ph.: 24694610; Fax : 24618637
www.indiaresearchpress.com
contact@indiaresearchpress.com; bahrisons@vsnl.com

2007

ISBN thirteen: 979-81-8386-035-2
ISBN ten: 81-8386-035-4

Printed for *Tara Press* at Focus Impressions, New Delhi-110003

To Vandana who strives through life's injustices with amazing grace

CONTENTS

1.

Whispers in the Wind

There was the immovability of mountains about that figure, but the eyes were a living stream, laughing, joyously alive. There was the darkness of brooding horrors about that face, but the lips had that special curve which only perpetual smiling bestows.

The eyes, wide as saucers, seemed to look through you and far beyond. You knew they saw everything but the lips gave away little. A hint of a whisper, or was it imagined? The doubt always nagged at your mind.

You left her but you always returned. The mysterious gypsy woman wrapped up in a cloak of gloom was an irresistible lure. Of course, part of the allure lay in that concealed crystal ball. She would look into it and her face would reflect its eerie colours. Shadows would chase each other across her face, losing themselves in the myriad wrinkles. Her expression would grow grim and you wondered what dark horrors in your life lay revealed before her. You would shiver and she would smile, tearing your heart apart.

Her face mirrored every mystery ever born. You would see huge forces at work – rivers in spate, storms in full blow, devastating earthquakes. You would want to flee, but, unable to move, oddly fascinated, you would remain. Besides, the music in your ears was too haunting for you to escape. It seemed as if doors and windows were just waiting to open out onto magic lands where nothing was impossible.

She would speak in strange tongues and gesture as if talking to invisible audiences, and you would be carried away, lost in the beauty of the magic words she would utter. You could almost imagine whispered echoes in reply. She would look at you and you would feel included in her charmed circle. A warm gratitude towards her would fill your soul, and then she would turn her face away and you were out in the cold again.

Sometimes you would laugh out aloud and the spell would be shattered. The gypsy woman would just look like any other tired woman and the smell of garlic and musty clothes would offend your nostrils. You would turn away, but the music of her pipe would play on your heart- strings and you would stay. The magic would return and her smile would beguile you with its shyness or slyness. You could never make up your mind. You would dance with her the magic jigs, and croon along with her when she sang to the moon. The stars would be shining pinpoints in a pitch black sky, throwing fairy lights on the heath where you danced, and the howling of wolves would set your teeth on edge.

You went with her to woods where magic still lives – where you spear the eye of a salmon with a silver spear. You climbed with her the highest mountains and plunged into the deepest seas. You went with her to the heart of all things, and you learnt to see beyond what others saw. You did all that and more, and there was sunshine in her eyes and home - come in her smile.

Somewhere along the road you tired of mysteries. The shadows grew dark and the way grew too long. The peaks remained unclimbed and the sea no longer called out to you. The gypsy woman did not speak out her mind, but there was a mute appeal in her eyes, which you did not see. She smiled less and less and soon she smiled no more.

Your life took you to other lands but one day you did return and your wandering steps took you to the old gypsy camp. You saw her tent in the distance. Frenzied winds lashed at her shelter and a lone coyote howled in abject loneliness. Forgotten by the world and you, she must have sung her dirges. But only a silent night would have listened and perhaps a lone star wept.

A terrible sense of loneliness assailed you as you entered the tent. She sat in a dark corner, a wan smile of welcome on her face. There was something about the smile, which chilled you. Somehow you knew she would never smile again.

She spoke to you of springs long past, of fierce summers, poignant autumns and winters of despair. She spoke to you in all the tongues she knew and you understood the meanings beyond the words.

She rose at length, and then began a dance you never would forget. She was as sinuous as a sixteen-year-old, as graceful as a swallow in flight. There was not a trace of age in the movements, beautiful beyond words. You stood transfixed. Something was passing and you wanted it imprinted indelibly on your memory. Your tears fell like a hot cascade, but you were not ashamed.

There were no bells tolling when you carried her out. No mourners either. The only music was that playing in your heart. It was the poignant strain of a gypsy lute on a still night, celebrating death.

Let your tears flow for the gypsy woman; she is lost amidst the stars. Brush your tears away gently for she lives among them.

Can you see her shabby tent far away in the distance? A single star shines above it and a wild coyote howls in the wind. And doesn't your heart howl, too, for your gypsy woman?

Alas. There is no gypsy woman, there is no lonely tent. There is no strange music in the wind. Only life lying there before you waiting to be dreamt.

Wake up and dare to dream, and if you are lucky, and the stars are right, the gypsy woman may choose to dance again.

*****

2.

The Frog and I

He glared at me balefully from beneath the rock. And then he jumped at me. It was like a tennis player at the net having a ball hit straight at him. He has to jump to one side. I jumped to my left baffling him. He landed on soft feet. I landed in slush.

Such was my first meeting with the frog, and it hardly endeared him to me. Nor, I admit, did I feel any love flowing towards me.

I may have been able to ignore him, had the damned frog not been able to speak.

"Piss off," were the first words I heard him croak.

I groaned. It was all suddenly too much for me. To be shipwrecked and abandoned on an island, with a talking amphibian may be your cup of tea, but the brew's a little too weird for me.

Deciding on direct action, I peed straight at the frog. I was gratified to see his eyes dilate with distaste. "You can't be too much of a guy with women", he said, eyeing me pointedly. It was his way of getting back at me. I did not rise to his bait. No pun intended.

I raised a threatening boot at him and was pleased to see him pale "Who'll tell you what to do, if I am a pancake?" he asked reasonably.

I sobered down. The frightful little bugger had a point. Some company, even a frog's was probably better than solitary confinement on the island.

Meanwhile, the frog having dived into a little puddle, had come out looking refreshed, obviously the acidity of pee had not been to his taste. I recorded this priceless piece of information for possible further use. I needed any weapon I could lay my hands on to dominate him, for the frog seemed master of his environment and I felt a rather useless Crusoe to this unlikely Man Friday.

"And now", announced the frog portentously, "I am ready to listen to your tale, so full of human interest. Spout forth, Mac Duff".

"I don't know what there is to say, you undergrown runt", I said, meaning to hurt. "I have never talked to frogs before. Do you talk to them, at them or down to them? I wish they had taught us in school".

The frog drew himself up to his full height of three inches, "Whoreson", he said, with impressive dignity. "Speak up or fuck up".

I chose the former alternative "I have no story worth the telling. I have been shipwrecked on this God-forsaken island. You happen to be the last chapter of my life."

"You will adapt", said the frog confidently. "I did".

"What, were you shipwrecked too?" I asked facetiously.

"No, you silly arse", said the frog.

"I was a human being once. But you can't be human and live here. No blinking way".

"How did you change?" I asked curiously and wanting to keep him in good humour.

"Metamorphosis, of course", said the frog, as if that explained all.

"Ah yes, of course", I agreed easily. "Attaboy", said the frog approvingly. "The moron moves to the top of the class".

I gave the frog's right ear a satisfying tweak. "Leggo", he yelled. "Brute – Sadist. I ought to report you to the SPCF". I tweaked the frog's left ear, and thereafter deposited him in the breast -pocket of my jacket. As a strategy to keep him quiet, it was quite effective.

I needed to think and I settled down under a giant tree, thankful for the shade. My thoughts were rudely interrupted by a strange sensation in the region of my chest. The damned frog had returned the compliment. He had peed on me.

But no, the ecstatic expression on his ugly face told a different story. The damned frog was orgasming blissfully on my chest.

"Toad", I cried with loathing, and he looked up in startled irritation", "Would you mind having your dreamy peccadilloes elsewhere?"

The frog was embarrassed but strove manfully to regain his equanimity. "Happens to a man, you know", he said gruffly. "Adolescence... Puberty, you know, all that stuff". I had to laugh. Frog was the most non-pubescent being I had ever met. "Frog, you were born old", I told him.

"I keep myself young with exercise", he replied. "Keeps me in fine fettle".

"That's moistly apparent", I said dryly. Frog had the grace to blush.

I gave him a not too gentle shove and froggie took the hint. With a prodigious leap he evacuated his cosy quarters, and proceeded towards a little pond, where I could hear him croaking rhythmically.

By and by I realised he was not merely croaking randomly. He was singing and his rendition could hardly have been less flattering to me.

"There he sits the little creep
Laughs because he cannot weep

Tight of sphincter, faint of heart
Can one humanise a fart?"

And as he sang each line he executed a joyful little leap in the air.

I decided to get my own back "Hey Frog", I yelled, "I can sing better". He stopped in disbelief as I broke out into song.

"Play you must and play you will
With your gonads, while there's life
The real test of froghood lies
In satisfying your frigging wife".

Froggle looked quite nonplussed and I could see him searching his mind for a snappy rejoinder.

"Toad", I said, pre-empting him. "Shut up".

"My name is not Toad, "he replied.
"Frog, then ", I said "or amphibian, if you prefer".

"My name is Grace," said the frog. I burst out laughing. "Don't be silly Frog. Capone is more likely, or Atilla in your nicer moods".

"I am a lady", said the frog, coyly. This was a new angle and it really threw me. The intellectual pressure of the conversation was getting a little too much for me now.

"Things are not what they seem", he confided.

"But why the disguise and all the prevarication?" I asked with indignation.

"Because a girl can't be too careful these days ", said the frog. "I was afraid of rape".

"But who would rape you?" I asked in genuine perplexity. "Have you ever seen anything more ugly?"

The frog's mouth twisted with hurt and he shot me a look full of strange pleading. I was suddenly ashamed of myself.

I was assailed by an overwhelming sense of loss. The convivial locker room bonhomie was a thing of the past. Frog was a damned dame!

"Sorry, Frog", I added, feeling rather like a novice done in by a card sharp. "I can still call you Frog, can't I?"

"What else would you call a frog, muttonhead?" said the frog, once more in command. This was the frog as I knew him, before all his coy simpering and confusion of sex.

I saw the frog's body beginning to shimmer and a terrible fear overcame me. "Metamorphosis?" I asked in a dreadful whisper.

Frog nodded dumbly and I could see him dissolving before my eyes. There was a look of desperation in Frog's eyes – a look I had never seen before in anyone's eye – not pleading, not mere regret, but a thousand may-have-beens.

The frog's face hung low in the air like a Cheshire Cat's smile, slowly disappearing.

I threw caution to the winds and I stepped up to him. Yielding to a sudden impulse, I implanted a swift kiss between the fading bulbous lips.

A thousand suns lit up the night and I was blinded. "My prince", said the apparition, and there was the smell of roses in the air.

*****

3.

Murder Most Foul

I sat atop a cliff overlooking a frozen sea. All the sadness in the world seemed to be lapping in these waters. I was a man in a Japanese painting, sitting at the edge of all things, hoping for a push, which would somehow restore sanity to a mad world.

A seagull suddenly appeared by my side, "Hullo seagull", I said full of gratitude for this apparition materialised to share my loneliness.

"Don't be silly", he said to me. "Seagulls don't speak".

"But", he continued, "I can. I am not a seagull, you see. I am an albatross, ignoramus. And albatrosses, as anyone knows, can speak." He looked at me pityingly.

" Ignoramus", he muttered again, under his breath.

"Ah", I said, seeing the light. "Like the one whose lights went out with a crossbow? But are you albatrosses or albatrix?"

"I, ignoramus", he said rudely, "am neither. I am an albatross. Singular, not plural". Clearly he wished to evade my question and I did not deem it politic to pursue this course of enquiry any further.

The albatross seemed to be getting quite agitated and I feared if I disturbed him too much he might take to hanging around my neck. And that was a prospect I did not particularly relish.

"Brother Albatross, singular", I said, pacifically, "What is your *raison d'etre*?"

"Keep it clean", said the bird in the clipped accents of a Chicago thug. "Your question is in extremely bad taste, *n'est ce pas*?"

Score one for the bird, I thought, and cursed Alliance Francaises all over the world. I lapsed into a moody silence, till finally the bird broke the pall.

"Don't sulk", he ordered with the air of one used to being obeyed.

"First things first", I said, trying to get my basics right. "Are you male or female?"

"I have never been so insulted in my life", said the albatross. "Female albatrosses don't intellect".

I didn't ask him to elucidate. He seemed disappointed and tried another tack. "They don't rap either", he said.

This time I rose to the bait. "You mean rap like in Eminem?" I asked him.

"No, rap like in this", screeched the bird triumphantly synchronising motion and speech. I drew back my bleeding knuckles. "Played you for a sucker", he chuckled wheezily.

I don't know if an albatross has ever rapped you. Believe me, it's not fun. My hand was a bleeding lump of raw meat, and remembering my fine, shapely hand from pre-albatross times, I shed bitter tears. I found myself wishing the bird would just fly away.

"Just like the mariner", he said, reading my thoughts. "No philosophy. Pain can be a great teacher".

"And look at you, "he went on. " A runaway from life. People don't do such things. It's not in good taste."

I didn't ask him how he knew my story. It was obvious he could read my thoughts.

"Don't even have the balls to marry", he said, rowelling in the spurs. "Unreal, adolescent, foolish." He seemed to relish every invective that he hurled at me.

"You have a wife Mac?"I asked him through clenched teeth, finally losing all patience.

The bird laughed as if at some private joke, "Killed her last autumn," he said blandly.

"How did you kill her?" I blurted out, startled at this strange confession.

The bird laughed nastily "I let her wither", he said. "I took away the love".

I felt a great surge of hatred shoot through me at the heartlessness of this terrible avian. The rage seemed to fill my mind and I found the bird could no longer read my thoughts, as it had been able to earlier. The all encompassing hatred I had developed for him seemed to have swamped his telepathic ability.

"You're not nice", I told him. "You're as rotten as last week's socks".

He seemed genuinely surprised "What's the matter? You don't like a winner. Huh?"

"No, I don't like your kind of winner", I found myself shouting at him. "And I sure as hell don't like you. Now get out."

I turned away from him to look at the dark sea and I saw the shadowy figure standing on the boat. "As idle as a painted ship upon a painted ocean". The words of the poem came unbidden to my mind and a terrible idea began to take shape in the labyrinths of my brain.

I knew it was meant to be and that nothing could prevent it – it was preordained and I was the instrument of destiny. I tried to hide the excitement that threatened to give me away.

I turned to the bird conversationally with the brightest of smiles "By the way", I asked him casually, "can albatrosses fly?"

"Why do you ask?" he queried suspiciously "Is it a hint to try and get me to leave? Why are we on speaking terms again? I thought I was not nice."

"It has nothing to do with niceness", I responded coldly, feeling like the executioner of Lille, the excitement rising in my throat. "I don't suppose those ungainly wings of yours serve any aerodynamic function. Just like the rest of you, I guess.... phony".

The look he gave me went past the unholy. "I know your little plan", he said, and I felt as if I'd been socked in the solar plexus. "You think you can chase me away with rudeness. No such luck".

I sank back with relief. I was far more diabolical than he had given me credit for. I goaded him again. "Female albatrosses can't fly, did you say?"

He didn't respond. "How come I didn't see you fly in? Crept in behind me did you, with a phony swoosh of wings? Hey bird, you can't fly", I said.

The bird looked at me enigmatically and the pride of Lucifer was in his eyes as he soared into the air in a beautiful arc and my breath caught in my throat at the glory of it.

I followed that graceful arc till the bird was nearly out of sight, and then I sensed, rather than saw, the inexorable verdict of doom pierce his breast at the height of his glory.

The twang of the crossbow came to my ears over the placid waters like a plaintive obituary.

I saw the figure in the boat raise his fist towards the sky and heard the frozen echoes of his triumphant shout.

I turned away feeling justice had been done, but I knew the mark of Cain had stamped itself indelibly on my soul. I had murdered in cold blood and something told me I would kill again.

*****

4.

Turn of Sabres

She was passion, she was wine. She was beauty, she was grace. She was everything a man could possibly have wished for. There was only one flaw. She was a murderess.

As the music grew more and more romantic and the couples on the dance floor huddled closer to each other, I knew I would have to denounce her very soon. The thought made me shiver and I wondered whether I would have the courage to go through with it.

She was a picture of innocence, laughing gaily, without a care in the world. And the entire world fawned on her. There was not a man in the room who would not have lain down his life at her glance. I was not sure I was an exception.

From time to time I could see her glancing at me over the shoulders of her constantly changing partners. There was such mockery in her gaze that I could feel my ears going red. Once, I even thought I saw her wink. But may be it was the wine...

Finally, the dancing couples came back to the table. It was a sight to warm the coldest heart. Strong men with sabres, dressed in scarlet and white, with ladies draped gracefully, like lilies, over their arms. It would be such a damnable fuss to drop the bombshell.

The couples seated themselves. Glasses were refilled and the liquor flowed freely. I could not but join in, and for some time was a part of the merriment.

She sat right opposite me and I could see the question in her eye. But there was no hint of remorse on her face, nor even a plea in her glance. What was she made of? I wondered.

The music resumed and she was whisked away again. She came back after a dance or two and sat right next to me. "Well, have you decided yet?" she asked without preamble.

"Decided what?" I parried.

"Oh don't be a bore", she said good - humouredly. "You know – whether to keep mum or to tell all."

"I don't see how I can help you", I said coldly.

"That's just it", she said. "You can't see", and with those enigmatic words she swept off into another dance.

She came back alone. "Will you, won't you, will you won't you, won't you join the dance?" she asked me laughingly. I could not but oblige.

Her body was pure gossamer against me and her eyes held the promise of spring. I felt myself surrendering to the magic of the evening and somewhere along the line I must have taken a decision. I remember hazily the goodbyes during the early hours of the morning and the promises to meet again.

She held a curious fascination for me and we met several times thereafter. But even through the various stages of intimacy, something kept me from total surrender. After all I had been a witness to horror and I could not forget. And something told me that I had forgiven or at last condoned an atrocity, which I had no right to do.

The days passed blissfully and I had almost succeeded in convincing myself that I had imagined it all, when she herself broke the spell. "Well, do you still hold me guilty of some terrible crime?", she asked me, suddenly, one day.

I felt afresh the horror of the moment and the emotion must have shown on my face. "I saw what you did", I blurted out. "It was cold - blooded murder".

Her laughter was bright and unaffected. "He was a mere pup", she said contemptuously. "It was a trifling dalliance. Naturally," she paused, "he had to die".

For the first time I could see through her laughing eyes and I was chilled to the bone. It was unreasoning madness I saw there. The murder of a human being counted as little for her as tearing petals off a bloom. A replacement would be found soon enough followed by another *coup de grace*. And now, my reasoning said, I was next. Was I a mere pup too? I wondered. Is that how she saw me?

I saw her look at me appraisingly and I could see the lust glaze her eyes. She caressed my chest. "But you are a man", she said, "And I need men".

She reached for me imperiously and in spite of myself I responded to her embrace. We were in the throes of love - making when there was the sound of strident knocking on the door.

I felt my passion subside as I hastily leapt for my clothes. I did not need to see the wolfish grin on her face as she ran to open the door. "Here he is", she shouted excitedly pointing me out to the six men who were entering the room.

The six sabres turned in the air, their edges glinting together like a burst of sunlight. But I was already diving out of the window where a horse waited to carry me to safety.

A sense of *deja vu* assailed my senses. I had to pinch myself for assurance that it was all happening, as it had, when I had witnessed the murder of that innocent boy.

I looked up to see her face seeking me in the darkness, but I could see in it only the innocence of lilies.

I could have ridden to safety but the moonlight suddenly fell on her face and I saw the transformation – the innocence was gone, revealing the stuff of which nightmares are made. No, it could not be, I swore to myself, and I rowelled the spurs cruelly into the sides of my horse as I galloped half-naked towards the house.

She held out her open arms to me invitingly. But the scream that issued forth from my throat was not human as I rode her down.

They are coming for me and I am sure they will get me. But I am content for I have just seen her, astride a silver broomstick, heading for the moon.

*****

5.

Cliff-Hanger

The figure, which stood atop the forbidding cliff outlined against the sky, had not moved for an hour. It had the immovability of a wild animal waiting with a terrible patience before it pounces on its prey. The watcher below had to focus his binoculars carefully to assure himself that the figure was indeed human, and not a statue carved out of rock.

And now he could see her face, brought close by the powerful lenses of his Zeiss binoculars. It was a face as stony as the cliff on which the figure stood. It had been a beautiful face once, he mused, with an emotion as near to pity as he was capable of. Those eyes had smiled, those lips had laughed. Time had its ways, he reflected cynically.

He had done his research well and he knew he was near the end of a twenty-year-old quest. There was only one way up the cliff, and only one – the same way – down. There was nowhere she could go. All the roads had run out.

He was in no hurry. The wait had been long and he wanted to savour every minute of what was certain to be a satisfying ending.

The man stood tall, dwarfing the Landrover, which had carried him thousands of miles in his savage quest for revenge. He wore an expensive looking suit, oddly at variance with his unkempt appearance. His eyes were bloodshot with lack of sleep – but his expression was a contented one – that of a jungle cat which has cornered its prey.

There was something about the woman's posture, which disturbed him. There was in it an odd readiness which he had seen somewhere. He laughed at his uneasiness. Nothing could save her now. He had killed the husband years before with a telescopic rifle. But that would be too easy. Someone had to pay for his grey years. He wanted her to know the end had come, to smell her fear, to see the horror in her eyes, to hear her beg.

If the woman was aware of his presence, she showed no sign of it. She continued to gaze out to sea, as if waiting for someone to return. He had observed her for a week and the routine had never varied. In another hour she would begin the descent.

He glimpsed some movement and it startled him, so motionless had the figure been. It was just the woman adjusting her shawl. His nerves were taut with expectancy, and he took a few deep breaths to calm himself down.

He forced himself to think back to the last time he had seen her, crouching like a wounded animal over her husband's dead body. He had wanted her to hurt and the granite face he had seen through the binoculars was evidence enough. The woman had suffered.

He squared his shoulders as a prelude to beginning the long climb. The North Wind howled a cacophony of curses at him as be walked up the cliff – towards the path from which only one would return. He was chilled to the marrow even under his heavy clothing. It was a wonder that the wind did not blow the slight figure on the cliff into the sea.

He walked slowly, his tread heavy with memories. He had no need to hurry, for no one was going anywhere. Time had suddenly stood still.

It was after an hour's steady climb that he finally reached the top of the cliff. The figure had not changed position and a superstitious dread clamped itself upon his heart. Was she dead, frozen into permanent immobility upon this dreadful promontory? Had he been cheated of his prey, the wine of victory snatched from his very lips?

The well - remembered voice sent his pulse racing. "I knew you would come", she said simply. "That it would be reduced to just you and me at the end of all things. It began with us. Thus must it end. Don't you see the simplicity of it all – the beauty of it?" She paused. "I have waited for you many long years."

The figure turned, drawing the shawl tightly over her shoulder as a little chill shook her. "Do what you have to", she said.

The man saw the ravaged face and the resignation in her look. Is this what he had travelled thousands of miles to see, given years of his life to? Was it really revenge he wanted? He felt totally emotionless as he gazed at her. This woman meant nothing to him.

But even so he must do what he had come to. He looked at her searchingly, but there was no pleading in her eyes; nothing that he could savour after her death. The man took a step towards her and she shrank back involuntarily. "I'm sorry", he said, "that it has to end this way."

She looked him in the eye. "He was always a better person than you. I'm glad I chose the right man".

The words hurt like nothing ever before had. He had not imagined anything would ever hurt him again. But he had been wrong. This implacable woman had driven hot nails through his soul.

He looked at her, molten rage flowing through him, and he knew he would strangle her with his bare hands. The thought gave him some satisfaction, and he resumed his walk towards her.

"I'm sorry, too", said the woman, throwing off her shawl. Her hand was steady as a rock as she shot him neatly through the heart. "You should have been more careful". She paused. "But then, you always were a fool".

He was dead before he hit the ground. But the woman had already turned away to resume her lonely vigil, staring out to sea. Much later, she turned, but there was nowhere to go.

She looked for a long while at the body at her feet, and then, quite deliberately emptied the remaining bullets into the still form. With a shiver of revulsion, she flung the gun far out to sea. The last act had been performed.

The whole universe lay open to her as she walked over the edge of the cliff, her arms outspread in wingless flight.

*****

6.

The Chosen One

The sun was orange against a leather sky, while the shaman lay dying in the desert. The dark figures which stood at his bedside had not moved for hours, in sharp contrast to the swiftly circling vultures, which sensed the end.

The dying man looked at the vultures and smiled. "Wait patiently, my friends", he whispered softly. "You will feast tonight." His face turned towards the assembled figures and he looked at them through a red haze. They were all there, several aspirants to the position of shaman of the tribe. It was the most powerful position imaginable, the most critical for good or for evil. Before this night, a successor had to be chosen.

He looked at the faces again. All seemed carved of stone. Not a glimmer of sympathy, not a human emotion. The old man sighed and looked away. The signal had still not come, but come it would. Generations of shaman had lain here at this very spot, and the sign had always been given. It was the way.

The old man closed his eyes and drifted off into sleep. He dreamt of several shamans before him, the last of who had been his mother's father.

His own father had been a warrior with scant interest in things spiritual. In fact, the father had been rather in awe of his son. The thought amused the dying man and he smiled in his sleep.

The crowd of watchers looked at him with concern, hoping he was not losing his mind. That would be tragic. Without a shaman the tribe would be lost, and he had yet to indicate a successor.

The hours passed slowly, until, mercifully, the orange haze gave way to an indigo night. The watchers drank the strong herbal brew that the squaws had prepared. No other food was permitted till the last rites were over.

The old man dreamt of his youth, of cold streams in which he had dived as a boy, of battles he had witnessed, of the folly and of the nobility of humans. And had it been worth it? The old man nodded in his sleep. The watchers saw the movement but could not understand it.

It was midnight when he opened his eyes. He was thirsty, so thirsty, but water was forbidden to him. To give him water would be to destroy the rite itself, and no one would dare to do that. The rule was an inexorable one, unquestioned since the beginning of time.

The old man felt the life beginning to seep out of him. The moon hung low in the sky like an anaemic sickle, pale and watery. Like me, thought the old man with a wry smile.

"Come close to me", he said in a surprisingly loud voice, and the watchers drew nearer to him. "It is time". What sounded like a sighing breeze was a collective letting go of indrawn breaths.

The would-be successors spoke in his ear. Many philosophies were outpoured, and he listened. Not a fraction of feeling did his face betray, as he judged them in the last hour of his life.

The faces darkened one by one as he bade them go. There were only three left now of a once large crowd. The rest of the watchers had withdrawn to a sullen distance.

The large man who approached the shaman had been his most faithful follower, and the shaman bestowed upon him a smile much as one does upon a favourite dog. The man stood at his bedside for a long while, and then shedding tears, he turned away. Both knew he was a follower; a leader, never.

And then before the startled eyes of all, one of the remaining two had run forward to the shaman's bedside and sprinkled water on the parched lips.

"Sacrilege", shouted the watchers. "This man must die".

They grew close in a tight circle, ready to slay. But the strength of the shaman's voice cowed them. "Back", he ordered. "Back, fools". Following a lifetime of obedience the crowd stepped back. "Come here, Strongbow", he said to the Chief, "Touch my lips. Is there any water on them?"

The Chief snatched his hand back in agony as the parched, burning lips scalded his palm. "There is no water here", he said shaking his head in wonder.

"But what did we see?" asked one of the watchers.

"Do not always believe what you see", said the shaman sternly. He paused. "You saw a human being, my people. And human beings are very rare".

The white shawl covering the shaman's body flew off like a great white bird and settled in a vice-like embrace on the shoulders of the young man who had been unable to endure the ancient's suffering.

The old shaman raised his hands in a final salute, and the new one found his own rising in acknowledgement.

*****

7.

Camelot

I heard their frenzied coupling amidst the ruins, the wild moans indicative of their primitive need. It was a passion that had to be satisfied, heedless of consequence. I wanted to go far away and leave them the dignity of privacy. But there was no way I could leave without announcing my presence. And that would have been fatal. Besides, I was a spy...

The woman spoke at length. "I know how you hate all this deception. But do we have a choice?"

The man's handsome face wore a haunted look, and his eyes did not meet hers. "We never did have a choice, Genevieve," he said gently.

"Arthur would never understand", she said, taking his head in her lap. "Arthur understands very little. He is so obsessed with form".

"That is not fair Genevieve", said the man gently kissing her. "Arthur is all that any one can hope to be. Arthur is perfect".

"Aye, that he is", said the woman bitterly "Too damn perfect. And perfect is complete in itself. Arthur requires nothing apart from himself".

The man looked at her pityingly. “It must be difficult”, he said at length.

The woman gathered her clothes around her with queenly dignity. “I must go”, she said.

“Must you, my queen?” asked the knight kneeling before her.

“Yes, my Lancelot. I am expected back for dinner. And you will be there.” She gave him a lingering kiss, sprang daintily atop her horse and galloped away.

I was left staring at the man’s unhappy face. Poor Sir Lancelot, I thought. Poor unhappy devil, caught in a no-win situation. I could see the noble face raddled with indecision. No wonder he went to battle in such frenzy, praying for a death that would release him from his guilt.

I took in his build and the muscular strength of him, and I knew defeat was not his fate. Such a man was doomed to fight and never lose.

I saw him pull himself together with a heroic effort. I saw the worry lift from his brow and the mighty heart transcend its worries.

“Tirra-Lirra-La”, sang Sir Lancelot. I felt ashamed of myself, so prone to self-pity, in the face of this noble fortitude.

I mounted my steed and followed him at a distance. Soon we neared Camelot, the home of all chivalry and our path lay along the bank of a river. A dark, narrow boat floated on the water and on it lay a pale corpse, a maiden with the face of an angel, her hair spread about her, very young in death. Sir Lancelot glanced at her and shook his head sadly. But nothing repressed him for long. "Tirra - lirra - la" he sang out again as he passed by his unknown devotee, the Lady of Shalott.

We reached Camelot, late in the evening. Sir Lancelot, being the champion he was, was warmly welcomed wherever he went, and I followed behind, at a respectful distance.

Suddenly there was a hush and I saw a noble figure approach, All those present bent their knees to the king. At his side was a virginal beauty who shone like the evening star. I could scarcely believe this was the Queen Genevieve, who only a short while ago I had witnessed in far less regal circumstances.

I saw Lancelot's face light up like a thousand suns and I wondered how long he would be able to conceal his passion.

The king came forward. "Lancelot, my Lancelot, where have you been? We have missed you, have we not, Genevieve?"

I saw the queen look up sharply at him before

replying, "Lancelot is always with us. Has he really been away somewhere?"

Lancelot bowed to the King. "I am touched by the King's concern and the queen's utter indifference". The royal couple laughed and the moment of awkwardness passed. I saw Lancelot clench his fists in an agony of despair and the queen bestowed upon him a loving glance, unnoticed by her lord.

The carnival went on and I saw the happy faces in a haze of dust and song. At length the night came to a close, and I saw the king draw Lancelot aside. I stepped behind a convenient tree to overhear, for such was my profession. I was curious as to what gems of strategy such warriors would debate.

"What gorgeous gems she has, the Lady Rowena, Lancelot. Wouldn't you like to squeeze the sap out of them with those monstrous hands of yours or give suck to those swollen nipples?" the royal monarch asked.

"No my lord, I prefer the Lady Samantha. She makes any gown look six sizes too short. Look how opulent she is", rejoined Lancelot.

"We could flip a coin for them", said Arthur pacifically.

"Nay, my lord, both are yours", said Lancelot

gracefully, quite the royal courtier. "I shall make do with a country wench. Besides, so much nobility would kill me".

I heard them both laugh, as they walked away arm-in-arm. Arthur saw Lancelot to his horse and then turned towards his palace. I was close enough to hear him mutter, "Genevieve never was a mere country wench my friend". There was more loneliness in that face than in the waters that lapped the most desolate Arctic wastelands. But the next moment he collected himself. Such is the way of kings.

I slunk away to deliver my report to my master. I could see the money glittering in his tight fist. I opened my mouth to speak and the reply surprised me. "Nothing to report", I said, and I heard his purse snap shut.

"Too bad", he said. "Too bad", I agreed, and thus ended our laconic conversation. Lest you think me noble, let me hasten to explain. I was in no danger of starving. I was a double and it was a rare day that I did not feast.

I tapped on Merlin's chamber and the wizard bade me enter. His eyebrows arched the question across to me. My report was the same as I had given earlier. "Nothing to report", I said.

"Oh happy day", exclaimed the magician. "Thy avarice is dead. Can it mean what I think?"

I nodded. "The boy is now a man, and every inch a king".

The magician looked at me enigmatically, and tossed me a huge purse. I caught it cleanly because of years of practice.

"Let him go", I said to the wizard, without looking at the gold.

"I just have", said the wizard. "You're fired".

*****

8.

Gun Fight At Tombstone

The old man had been fast, real fast – faster with a gun than anyone in Texas. It was rumoured that the Earps had given him a wide berth and that as sheriff in several countries, he had kept the peace simply because it was known that you ended up in Boothill if you tangled with him. It was also said that there were twenty-one notches on his gun.

When you asked to see his gun his reply was always the same: "Come and get it". No one dared to take up the challenge. It was said he still kept his hand in at the abandoned old quarry in his ranch. But he never spoke about it. It was as if he had buried his gun with his badge.

The old man had had a mother whose favourite saying had been: "Those who live by the sword perish by it". He had taken the teaching to heart, and he knew it was equally true of a gun. He had seen too many good people die to doubt its truth.

He had raised a God - fearing family and had seen to it that his children had received a good Christian education. Gun-fighting, he told them, was a sucker's game. There was always someone faster. And there were no survivors. And that was "Pop's law", as his kids put it.

His children had never seen him fight and his wife would never speak about it. He would not be drawn when he was asked about his gun-fighting days. He would just shake his head gently, giving no offence to his questioners.

The older people, of whom there were now only a few left, still talked of him. "Faster than Wyatt? I don't know. But Wyatt was certainly in no hurry to find out", one would say. The others would guffaw at this. It was a tale told and re-told.

The old man ran a respectable saloon. The liquor was good, the gambling fair and the girls lovely. With his reputation to add spice to things, the place was a roaring success.

The years passed. The children grew up, and the old man was now nearly seventy-five. It was an age at which he had reached serenity. Things of the past had been long since buried. But the past has a way of catching up with you unexpectedly.

He was returning from Church one morning when a hand pushed him from behind. The old man went sprawling on the sidewalk.

"Chicken", said the young man towering over him. "Plain bloody chicken".

The old man picked himself up from the

ground. "What's the matter?" he asked. "Why the rough stuff?"

"Lousy murderer", screeched the youngster. "You killed Kit Hudson without giving him a chance. You shot my father in the back. "

"I never shot anyone in the back", said the old man with dignity. "I never needed to. He was killed in a crossfire. Kit was my friend".

"Liar", screamed the youngster hysterically. "Get yourself a gun and I'll show you".

The old man shook his head, "I don't wear a gun. No use for it". But the boy was rife for trouble.

"I'll see you at six this evening in front of your saloon. If you have the balls, come with a gun. Else I'll brand you chicken clean across Texas."

The old man looked at him levelly. "I never ran away from a fight, son. I'll be there. But I'd be happier if you didn't come". Before the dumbfounded boy could reply, the old man had walked away.

The whole town was agog with excitement. They had heard of the old man's gun - fighting skill. But he was all of seventy-five years old, several decades past his prime. And the boy was tough and rode with a hard crowd. It was an unfair fight.

It was on the sixtieth second after five fifty-nine that the old man made his appearance. He looked frail and worn and the crowd half feared that the breeze would blow him away. They noted that his gun belt hung low in the tradition of the true, fast gunfighter, and his arms were poised at a comfortable distance from his guns.

The youngster saw him coming and looked more than a little surprised. "Well, well, if it ain't old Father Time himself. Hope you haven't forgotten to wind your watch for the last time?", he said with funereal humour, raising a titter from his companions.

The youngster could not resist goading the old man further. "That gun there looks like Colonel Colt's first invention," he taunted.

"Actually, you're not far off", said the old man conversationally. "It was his third. He made it specially for me. I've modified it some".

The youngster felt as if someone had just walked over his grave. "I was just joking," he said gruffly.

"I know", said the old man. "But I wasn't". The youngster saw the old man dressed in black standing before him, tall and unafraid and the beginnings of doubt assailed him.

"I don't want to kill you", said the youngster.

"Just admit you're chicken. That's good enough for me".

"You'll have to do much better than that," said the man in black. "You're getting no false confession out of me."

"You stupid old man", snarled the youngster. "I'm giving you a last chance. Admit your guilt or draw".

The old man did neither. He continued to walk towards him, narrowing the distance. "Draw when you want to", he said casually.

The young man watched him approach with a kind of macabre fascination. And then suddenly went for the gun in his left holster, in what he thought was a blur of motion.

The old man's draw beat him by miles, and the youngster found his holster with his undrawn gun cut clean away by a bullet which creased his left thigh. The audience gaped at the speed and the deadly aim of the old gunfighter. No one had seen his hand move.

The youngster braced himself for the bullet, which would surely end his life. "Come on and get on with it," he snarled, "Kill me".

"You're not half the man your father was",

said the old man. "I didn't kill him and I have no fight with you."

The youngster could only gape at him. But the old man was not looking at him. He had holstered his smoking gun and was walking away.

Someone in the crowd heard him mutter. "Too damned old for this. My old lady was right, you need nerve to kill a man. Should have plugged him in the navel. Bloody coward. It's time to hang up your guns when you start to shoot fancy".

He was still muttering to himself, when he turned back and absentmindedly shot off the shivering youngster's second holster.

*****

9.

The Last Southern Lion

The age of dinosaurs was coming to an end. The ice had taken a heavy toll and mammoth carcasses were strewn all over the earth. The smaller animals had managed to find shelter in caves and, had thus survived. But if the world did not thaw out soon even those animals would go the way of their larger brethren.

Roarer the king of the Southern Lions and his wife Fury had clawed their way to a spacious cave, where Fury settled down to deliver her cub. It was the first time she was giving birth and her anxiety was enormous. The Southern Lions were near extinction and her cub would be the only one of its generation for many hundreds of miles. It was essential all should go well.

Claw the Vixen had been appointed to perform this important task for she had delivered a hundred cubs in her day, and she knew more about midwifery than any other animal. But Fury's anxiety was beginning to set her nerves on edge.

"Be still, Fury", she growled in irritation, ignoring the wicked glance the lioness threw her way. She could get away with this curtness, the forthcoming birth was too important and the lioness helpless and dependent. But it was not wise to be too cheeky with royalty and Claw was aware that she had not been wise in expressing her irritation.

"It will be a king among cubs", she added unctuously and was reassured when the lioness smiled. Claw gave an inaudible sigh of relief.

The labour was long and the lioness writhed in pain. Claw stayed by her side, her face lugubrious and her demeanour calm as she tried to ignore the sounds of the nervous pacing of the anxious lion outside the cave. And then, after what seemed an interminable wait, there came a lusty roar.

Roarer wheeled around and pushed his great head through the opening of the cave. His face shone with pride. Fury smiled weakly at him, but it was a satisfied smile, the smile of a winner.

Claw smiled grimly to herself. She knew what her fate would have been if it had been a stillbirth. But she would have fought all the lions in the world for her life. She was made that way.

Wearily, she made her way out. "Leave them alone", she hissed at the king of lions. "She needs rest".

"Thanks", growled Roarer gruffly. "Your reward is waiting for you".

Claw did not even acknowledge the statement. She was headed for the forest for a quiet weep. Birth always affected her that way. Later she would eat...

She heard footsteps following her. "What is it now?" she asked testily. And then it struck her. "Oh it's a boy", she said.

The father smiled sheepishly, his heart swelling with pride. "That's what I had assumed, "he said lamely.

"Oh go catch a duck", said Claw irreverently and walked away into the jungle. Roarer did not react. He was used to women and their hysterical ways.

In the jungle Claw wept uncontrollably till all the tension had oozed out of her body. The vixen then shook herself out of the mood. She raced through the forest mindlessly, not caring where she was heading, until she dropped down exhausted. She chose a shady spot to rest and was soon fast asleep. Tonight she would feast.

She woke up quite frozen. Snow was falling and she knew she had to find shelter soon. She headed back for the cave where she had left the new mother. The lioness was awake. But the baby was snoring gently. "What a fine cub", said Claw, as she had said a hundred times before. Fury smiled at her, like every new mother, believing her cub the most wonderful ever born.

A sharp hoot startled them both. Claw turned around to see Delphi the Owl perched upon a ledge in the cave. "Aye, he will indeed be a great king". Claw eyed him with jealous disfavour.

"The bird knows nothing", muttered Claw under her breath.

"I heard that", said the owl, "It is not I who speaks, but the Oracle".

Fury crossed herself with superstitious dread. "Quiet, Claw", she commanded, wanting to hear more. Claw subsided into sullen silence.

"His life will be full of great deeds, and he will be a mighty king". The mother's eyes shone. "But", continued the bird, "He will be the last of the Southern Lions". And with an ominous flutter of wings, the owl departed.

Fury felt a cold stone settling down in her heart and she was filled with a nameless dread. Nothing Claw could say would comfort her, and dark forebodings filled her thoughts.

It was thus that Roarer found her when he entered the cave. "What's the matter Fury?" he asked, puzzled. "I thought we were rejoicing".

Fury did not have the heart to tell him. "Nothing", she said quietly. "I am just tired".

"Don't lie to me, woman, "said Roarer. "You look like the coming of the Ice Age". And so she told him.

Roarer had little respect for owls. "Don't you listen to that bird-brain. He doesn't know his crest from his toes". But she was not comforted.

The feast lasted the whole night long and Claw got quite drunk on the carnage. It was her way of forgetting. But the words of the owl had cast a shadow and darkened her mood and she saw the unhappiness Fury tried vainly to conceal. The owl did not join the feast.

Fury continued to brood and Claw watched her turn from her ebullient self into a surly, withdrawn recluse. Roarer worried too, but there was nothing he could do.

Claw saw the change in Fury and it hurt, because Fury was the closest to a friend that the vixen had ever had. It was all Delphi's fault, but there was little that could be done about it. Or was there? Claw was not one to wait and watch without acting.

The owl flew back to its nest that night to find it empty and its piteous hoots echoed through the forest. Claw smiled grimly to herself. Soon the search would begin. But Claw knew the forest like no other and she was confident it would be fruitless.

The days passed and the beating of the owl's wings grew more frantic as its search proved fruitless. Finally in desperation he came to Claw. "Claw I beg you, help me find my young ones".

"I fear you are the last of your tribe", said Claw sepulchrally. "These things happen you know. I am surprised you did not foresee this with your penchant for prophecy". There was a sly smile on the vixen's normally bland face.

A terrible understanding began to dawn on the owl and a wild hope arose within his heart. "Will you help me, Claw?" he begged.

"Perhaps", said the vixen meaningfully.

Roarer was delighted to see Fury emerge from her cave later that day, her eyes shining as they had so many moons before.

"It was all a mistake", explained the lioness. "Delphi came to see me and apologised. He had his constellations mixed up. Our child shall have many children. He will be a great warrior and our tribe shall live forever".

"I told you, you should never have listened

to that owl," said the lion. "He has caused us great harm with his foolishness." He looked at Claw. "Let's celebrate tonight".

It was a magnificent feast and each animal brought an offering. Claw was the last to arrive and she handed her gift to Roarer.

Fury saw him close his eyes in ecstasy as his strong white teeth tore into the gift. Horror struck her as realisation dawned. Fury knew that the only thing that affected him in that way was the flesh of a certain bird.

Fury glanced at her friend and the angelic smile on the vixen's face told her what she would never hear spoken. Even as she tried to suppress the dread that threatened to overwhelm her, she knew she would never see Delphi again.

*****

10.

A Trifle Too Late

We had been the greatest of friends once, as close as shadow to skin. There was nothing we had not shared from clothes to childhood experiences. On countless days we had played together from dawn to dusk and parted reluctantly to go to our respective homes.

Life in small towns can be idyllic. There were no villains to spoil the fun and several summers passed joyfully. And then came change. My friend slipped behind in his school work, and I went on to the next class.

It seemed a trifling thing to happen, but no, life is relentless. The same class is not just a loose group, it is much more, it is a clan. We could not realise this then.

We drifted apart, each involved in our separate worlds. Our meetings grew less and less frequent until a perfunctory nod was all that passed between us. Somewhere there was a pain. Maybe he felt it, too. Even today I am not sure if either of us was to blame. Circumstances can sometimes be too strong for the wisest among us, and we were only boys.

We competed against each other in sports, as boys will, and for some reason I cannot fathom, an unspoken animosity sprang up between us, each vying to outdo the other. It got so bad that we would not even speak to each other or acknowledge the other's triumph.

But boyhood passes swiftly and we grew up. I left the town to seek a career, but he remained. I still do not know what he does, but I often think of him and wonder whether we can be friends again. It is a foolish wish for a middle - aged man. Thirty years cannot be ignored. I wonder whether he thinks, too, of a friend he once had, and how foolish it is to let a thing as precious as friendship slip away.

I went back to that town one day, taken there by work. The meeting finished early and I decided to walk down memory lane. How well I remembered the massive steps that led to their front door.. The faces of his father, mother, brother were as clear to me as if it were yesterday. A great need to make amends suddenly came over me and I felt greatly virtuous as I made my way towards their house.

I was only a few paces away from those steps when the doubts began. Who would I find there? What would I say? His mother and father may have died. And he, would he welcome my visit? How would I explain it?

Conscience drove me on, but good sense made my steps drag. One can't just drop in after a thirty-year absence and say, "Tinkerty - tonk. I was just passing this way". What can you say? I had no answer, but I continued my walk. Soon I would be on the first step leading up to the house.

A light was on in the front room, as dim as it used to be so many years ago, or was it the failing vision of an aging man? The quality of light depressed me, and I felt an unbearable sense of self-pity, regret that I was no longer young.

I found myself climbing the steps reluctantly like a prisoner heading for the gallows. But finally I reached the front door.. The father's name had been replaced by the son's and a sense of foreboding overcame me. My hand held back from ringing the bell. Suppose a ghost appeared...

I'd come this far and felt compelled to continue. With an effort of will, I rang the doorbell. I was relieved to hear a young voice call out. "Who's there?"

"A friend of your father's," I replied, hoping I sounded at ease.

"Just a sec", said the voice and the door opened. The face at the door was my friend's, the voice just as friendly.

"Dad's not home", said the boy. "Nor is Mum - won't you come in?"

I sighed with relief. A reprieve. "No, another time", I said.

"Won't you leave your name?" he asked politely.

"Rip van Winkle", I replied, and the boy responded with a smile.

"No, your real name", he said.

"Tell him Old Father Time called", I said in jest and turned to go. But the boy insisted and so I left him a visiting card.

My heart beat fast as I climbed down the steps to leave, the feeling of relief overshadowed by a nagging sense of defeat. Mission unaccomplished. I felt like a thief leaving the scene of a crime. It was an irrational feeling for I had come out of good fellowship, to try to do a decent thing. Why, then , did I feel sneaky? Was it because I had tried to raise old ghosts and was relieved when the ouija board did not call up the resident spirit? Or was it because I did not feel competent enough to deal with the past? Was I, a man of forty or thereabouts, not mature enough to laugh at the carelessness of children? A man with a burden of ...guilt ? The answer, I suppose, is probably a little of all of these.

Later in the day my one-time friend will gaze perplexed at the business card of a life insurance agent who once tried to sell me a policy.

*****

11.

The Aftermath

The applause was still sounding in his ears as he walked away. As always, he was reframing the speech he had just made into the one, which should have been. It was such a pity not to get a second chance. One always blew the first, but audiences were not as critical as they might be, and one usually got away with it.

How much did people really understand, he wondered, of what was said, or pay attention to, for that matter? He knew his own attention strayed wildly and often. Probably other people were much the same.

A mile down the road the tension eased out of him and he was aware of an emptiness within. It always came to him, this feeling of emptiness, of not belonging after he had been in a crowd.

His thoughts went back to school – the brilliance and the athletic prowess, but had he ever bothered to revisit his Alma Mater. To go back to what? To empty classrooms and playing fields? To what applause? To what memories? He had been called a brilliant scholar and a credit to the school. But a school is really only a moment, an instant, the present. A school is cruel and it forgets. Five years later you are a myth, more improbable with each retelling. After ten years you are history. Fifty years later they hold a memorial service for you, if you are distinguished enough.

He had never really felt a part of any thing. Perhaps it was the fact that his brother and sister were a lot older and much of the time he had felt excluded from their world. In school, his brilliance distinguished him from his fellows. An outsider by circumstance, his essential non-belonging drove him to the limelight, to become the very spirit of every institution he ever attended.

It was the same through University and his professional degree; he was the golden lad wherever he went, in the centre of it all, so very afraid of not being part of anything.

It's strange, he thought, that I've managed to turn myself into an institution wherever I've been. Almost as if I was afraid of being lost, as if I wanted to create permanency.

"Am I so afraid of oblivion?" he wondered. One can only be afraid of something being lost if one possesses it? Have, I, therefore, always shunned possession? What kind of person really belongs?

Not my kind, he reflected wryly, as he continued walking. Even my family feels I am different, that I belong to another generation. But I did not belong even to that, he mused. What was I? What am I? The questions hit him with the force of adolescent doubts, surprising him with their intensity.

I was a seeker after truth, he said to himself. No, that sounds a little too trite doesn't it? Perhaps marching to a different drum sounds better. Yes that's it. I marched to a different drum. Or at least I tried to.

I wanted to be myself, but that is so difficult. The world does not let you. It labels you, and you spend your life stuck with it. To lead, you must be invisible. The logic is remorseless.

"Is that what I've tried to be?" he muttered aloud. "Invisible? And have I succeeded so well that it frightens me?"

"It's true I cannot see myself any more. There is no corner of me, which I can call my own. I reflect everything I have been a part of. Even my gestures are imitated, unconscious reflections of others. I am in danger of becoming a chameleon".

The man was troubled by his thoughts and his stride quickened automatically to keep pace with a wildly working mind.

"I must rediscover my essential self", he said aloud. Several decisions ran through his mind, and his mood lightened.

The lecture he gave the next fortnight was the best of his life. The distinguished gathering was on its feet clapping for his oratorical brilliance. The congratulations were heart-felt and sincere and he felt a warm glow. Once again he felt the sense of victory, of having put one over the audience, of being larger than life and therefore worthy of existence.

"He is the very essence of our field". The remark from the audience was the final affirmation of his brilliance.

He looked at the speaker with a studied mix of confidence and modesty, acknowledging the compliment with the air of a man who deserved no less.

"Thank you for your kind words", he said. The chameleon was already changing colour.

The walk back home was pleasant. The lecture he delivered to an imaginary audience far outdid in brilliance the one he had delivered at the auditorium. The bows he executed in enthusiastic acclaim of his own performance were far deeper than those he had made on stage.

A crowd of children passing saw a man clapping loudly in the middle of nowhere, but they were not unduly surprised. They were used to seeing drunks and madmen....

*****

12.

Quarry

The woman was very good at covering her tracks, but she was no match for him. He had spent forty-five years in the trade of deception, and he had learnt a lot about human cunning, more than most people learned in several lifetimes. But full credit to the woman, the way she went about it. Only a seasoned professional could have followed her the way he did. Not her poor husband, certainly.

He laughed at the thought and pictured the face of the husband, bloated and gross. Not for the first time, the contrast between husband and wife hit him forcefully. The woman was a beauty; the husband an absolute soak. He reflected philosophically on the mismatch, and his thoughts were not pleasant.

He had a job to do, and he went about it with cold efficiency. He had kept a diary of her movements for over three months. It recorded every infidelity committed by her, its time and duration. This neither amused nor disgusted him. His knowledge of human nature, gained from painstaking observation, was profound and he had long since ceased to judge people – they always had hidden motivations.

Meanwhile, he had to earn a living and this is what he knew. There are harder ways to do it than by following people.

The woman had entered a small brick house on a narrow street, and he bought himself a newspaper, prepared for a long wait. She was gone for two hours and when she stepped out onto the street again, she had a young man with her he had never seen before. He wrote a description of the man in his diary, unhurriedly and exactly. It might mean something to the husband.

They hailed a taxi and he did a "Follow that cab", routine in time worn style. They were headed for the sea front. What was the woman up to? He wondered. She had never ventured out so openly with anyone before. Was something about to give? Was she finally running away? News of that to the husband might mean a larger bonus. His heart beat a little faster at the thought.

But he reminded himself that his brief was only to follow her and report her movements, not to restrain her in any way. He was not the type to exceed his brief.

The taxi stopped at a waterside restaurant and the couple went in. It was lunch time and he resigned himself to another long wait.

They came out again much sooner than he had

expected and he managed to duck into a doorway before they saw him. Not that she would have recognised him, anyway. She had never seen him and did not know who he was. But he did not take chances.

He followed them till it was dark. They did not seem to have a definite purpose as they strolled casually, looking at the sea and the fashionable shops scattered along the water front.

Finally, he decided to eat at one of the smaller restaurants which gave a clear view of the street. Once, he almost panicked when he thought he had lost them but his experienced eye found them again and he chuckled. He was too old a hand to be taken in by them.

He finished his meal in a leisurely manner, forgetting about them for a while, confident that he would be able to pick up their trail without much difficulty. But it was getting very dark and the quicker he picked up their scent the better.

As he stepped out of the restaurant, he walked straight into a woman. His heart lurched. It was her. "I'm sorry", he blurted out, disturbed for a moment and not at all sure that it had been his fault.

"Oh, don't worry," said the woman. "I'm all right. I'm sorry", she added lamely.

"No,you are hardly to blame", he brushed

her apology aside. The woman smiled at him and then she offered him his precious diary which she held in her hand. "Is this yours?" she asked. He wanted to snatch it from her but instead he thanked her with steely control and added apologetically, "They're my grocery accounts. The wife insists on it". He managed to look convincingly embarrassed.

The woman laughed. It was an attractive laugh and the man was conscious of her extreme beauty. She turned and walked away.

He took a deep breath and began shadowing her again, a task made easier by the comfortable pace at which she was walking. She was alone, parted from the young man for the time being, and seemed to be window-shopping, peering into the more fashionable shops which catered to the well - heeled.

An hour more of dogging her steps and the old sleuth decided that nothing more of interest to him was going to happen that night. Just as he had decided to relax and perhaps go home for the night, the woman suddenly broke into a staccato trot on her expensive high heels and turned into a dark, deserted alley. He became aware of shabby buildings that housed the offices of down market solicitors and estate agents. Very curious now, his pace quickened to match hers as he moved along in the shadows.

She entered an empty undertaker's office and he followed her in cautiously. He peered around, trying to adjust to the darkness. His eyes were beginning to adjust to the gloom when a match flared, making his heart stop. The woman stood a few feet in front of him, looking at him. She had a diary in her hand.

Then what was it that he held in his own hand? As realisation dawned, he felt his skin crawl. The woman smiled as he opened the book he held and read the detailed record of his movements, moment by moment, over the last three months. She had switched diaries when she had bumped into him outside the restaurant. She had beaten him at his own game.

But there was more to come, he knew from the manic gleam of excitement in her eyes.

A noise from the street made him look around to see the obese husband entering the room, a broad grin plastered over his bloated face. The woman, too, had moved closer to him without being noticed. He was slipping up.

"You win", said the husband, as he embraced her. The woman laughed triumphantly, the laugh of a hyena.

The woman crooked a finger at him, beckoning him and the thought of disobeying her simply did not enter his mind. He followed her as he had for months, but this time not covertly.

She led him to a shadowy corner of the room and he shuddered at the sight of a plaque with his name engraved on it. He knew it was useless putting up a fight and slid, almost gratefully, into the empty coffin beneath the plaque. The last words he ever heard were the woman's, plaintively asking her husband, "When can we play this game again?"

*****

13.

Eternity

It was good to be back in the city where I had spent my boyhood. One can wander where one wants and become whatever one has to become, but a homecoming is always special, even when you have no home there any more.

Doors long closed to memory flew open. There was a sweet sadness in it but it was so much more real than wandering about the world looking for meaning, for reasons to live.

Childhood is a simpler time, meanings are not important, experience direct and not dissipated by sophistication. Things are seen as they are; an ugly face is called ugly, certainly not "interesting".

It was reflections like these that took me from my hotel to the very gates of the house, where more than fifteen years before, my childhood had been spent. I could not resist looking in.

Somehow, the huge mansion I remembered had shrunk. The passing of years has a way of doing that to memory. The house was clearly more run down, the ravages of time had discoloured it to a dirty yellow from the pristine white I had known.

I stood looking at the house, remembering happier times, images tumbling out, one after the other. I suppressed a yearning to enter the house. What would I see? And did I really want to see strangers desecrating the familiar? Did I want to compete with others for what had once been mine? Could grandfathers be conjured out of thin air? Would my mother smile at me again?

No, it was all very silly. I turned away but I was more than a little shaken by this brush with the past. So much had happened since I was last here. I thought of myself as level-headed and not unduly sentimental, yet I was unsettled by this look at the past.

I wanted to get away from this place where I had once been so happy and unwittingly my feet led me to a well remembered lane where I had once walked with my grandfather, trotting along beside him to keep up with his long strides. I smelt the early morning air again, the trees shedding their leaves in splashes of autumnal colour and the sky bursting into sunrise. The world stretched out before me, new and washed in exciting colours.

I walked at a furious pace to try to return to the present but this seemed to be my day for nostalgia. My steps led me to a large brick house with a lovely lawn. Memories of cricket and magnificent lunches brought tears to my eyes, and I had rung the bell on the gate before I could stop myself.

I asked for my childhood friend and was told he was out of town, but that his sister was in. Did I wish to meet her? Yes, I said automatically, and gave my name.

The smile that greeted me was pure sunshine. "Hello," she said. "You've been a long time coming".

"As if you've been waiting," I replied, and we both laughed at the absurdity of the exchange.

I learnt that my friend was now a prosperous doctor. I remembered his sister as a little irritating girl who would hide our cricket ball and only give it back to us after being promised sweets.

"And what have you been doing during these long years?" I asked her.

A shadow crossed her face. "Oh nothing much. Went to University, got married, lost a husband. I live here now". She said it all in one breath and the full implication of her words took a moment to sink in. "I'm sorry", I finally blurted out.

"Don't be", she said. "He was quite a rotter".

I left it at that. We spoke of old friends: she had kept in touch with many of them. I realised a part of my past had lived on quite independent of me and I was glad that all of it had not been lost . If

I worked hard enough, perhaps I would be able to salvage some portion.

The rational side of me told me to move on, not to be sentimental looking for a vanished past. But I still yearned to recapture something of myself from that time. Perhaps I wanted to reassure myself that my journey through boyhood had not been so trivial as to have passed without trace, to know that I too had left an indelible mark on those times.

Her mother appeared and made the usual fuss old women do. How strong and handsome I had become. I could not meet the young woman's eye but I could swear she was laughing softly to herself. Only after I promised to return in the not-too distant future was I allowed to leave.

It had been a pleasant encounter and, as I walked away, I became aware that I had laid some of the phantoms of the past to rest. I felt cleansed, as if I had purified myself of the effect of long buried emotions and I was suddenly glad that I had made this pilgrimage.

The girl's smile stayed with me all the way to the hotel. I had not seen the mother's nod of approval or the girl's silent acquiescence. I was still a stranger to the ways of women and did not know then that the past had ensnared me and it was even now shaping my future.

*****

14.

Houses

He had spent his whole life lusting for the house, and now it was his – a dream come true. The keys were in his hands, and in a few seconds he would enter it. He stopped suddenly, wanting to savour this long awaited moment.

The beautiful lawns held such memories for him. He recalled the tea parties and saw again the children from his young days, now grown up and gone away, The sister and brother who had lived here had both been his friends. Had they known he yearned for their house with every fibre of his being? No, probably not. They would have been surprised and probably repulsed by the intensity of his desire.

In the end, he had won and speculation was now irrelevant. The house, with all that it meant to him, was his. Every memory tied to that house was his.

In that moment he felt powerful, owner of everything that had ever happened here. He would reinvent the past, will it to be different.

He walked up to the front door and turned the key, and time stood still. He held his breath as he stepped into the hallway of the house he had paid a fortune to possess.

It was exactly as it had been, the gracious sweep of the long hall that lead to the dining room, the drawing room, the children's rooms. Nothing had changed. He was re-entering his childhood, threading his way through cobwebs and memories.

He lost all sense of time and it was only the onset of night that forced him back to the present. As he stood in the darkening hall an idea came to him. He would bring the past to life again and share his memories with others.

The party he gave was the event of the year for the townsfolk. They all turned up. He recognised faces from his childhood and old stories were swapped. His confidence grew as the evening faded into night and he felt master of the house.

Like birds of ill-omen they came at midnight. There were three of them, an old man and a girl and a boy, probably his son and daughter; they all had the same proud look and he felt the shock of familiarity. They ignored his welcome and walked purposefully into the hall.

"Isn't it dreary?" asked the young woman. The young man nodded. "I didn't realise it was such a dump." The old man glared at them. "Be civil, both of you".

"Don't listen to them", he said. "They really loved this place once". He looked at his host solicitously. "But you have your work cut out for you. There certainly is a lot to be done".

"I must confess", he continued, "that I was curious to know who had bought this place. But I don't think I know you, or do I?"

"Of course you do, Dad", said the young man and woman in unison. "He is our host". They both chuckled. They made themselves comfortable in the drawing room, just as they had thirty years ago, each in their own special place.

"Won't you have something to drink?" asked the girl.

"Or would you rather try some of this chicken?" offered her brother.

"Give him some soup", said the old man. "Or a drink if he prefers one".

The other guests had begun to leave and as they passed, they nodded in thanks to the three who sat so contentedly in the drawing room.

Time ran backwards and he was once again a guest in this house. His effort at playing host, at being master, had been a sham. It no longer felt like his house.

A sense of unreality gripped him and he felt that instead of a house, he had inherited a graveyard – his own perhaps?

He wanted to speak, to explain himself, but the expressionless faces of the newest arrivals were like waxwork images, uncaring and unmoved.

He rose to his feet but they did not look at him. They were chatting with each other, at home and oblivious of him. He could see they had kicked off their shoes.

He was the outsider, without purpose and unwanted. The party was over and he would have to go.

Three pairs of eyes suddenly turned on him, and he could feel their collective gaze bore through him. He heard himself saying good night and sensed rather than saw their gracious nods as he turned to leave.

It was the peals of vicious laughter that echoed through the house that finally unnerved him and startled him out of his trance. He dared not look behind as he ran in terror from those jealous phantoms. He was not used to such exertion, his heart was weak and his end inevitable.

"Is he dead?" asked the girl incuriously.

"Yes", said her brother and picked up something shiny from the floor.

The old man held out his hand for the keys and the three turned back to reclaim the house they had never left.

*****

15.

Candlelight

The man and woman lay on the beach in companionable silence, their love untarnished by eons. Each knew the other better than self; there really was no need to speak. When either spoke, the other was inevitably startled.

So the words of the woman jolted him from his deep reverie. "What a beautiful baby", she exclaimed, breaking the silence of millennia.

"Baby, what baby?" he had asked astonished. "Didn't we use that damned stuff? It was guaranteed to last a millennium or two. In any case, we are too young to have babies. We are only three eons old – not responsible enough yet".

The woman laughed throatily and pointed to a baby a few metres away, lying on the beach. "Look at his eyes - the eyes of Merlin."

"Balderdash", said the man. "Merlin was a grey beard, I don't think he was ever a baby."

"Gargle - goo", said the baby, his blue eyes fixed on the man.

"Farty-poo", said the man facetiously, scowling back. The words were scarcely out of his mouth when the baby executed a kind of somersault and landed squarely on his stomach. The breath went out of him in one swift whoosh.

The woman laughed. "Serves you right for mocking at wizards. Lucky you're half faerie or that may have been the *coup de grace.*"

"Bosh", said the man, looking around for the baby who had mysteriously disappeared again. No, there he was, a hundred metres away. "Fast crawler, eh?" he asked his mate.

"Did you actually see him move?" she asked, looking at him pityingly. "That is Merlin".

"Don't be silly", said the man, beginning to get annoyed." Everyone knows that Vivienne's spell has cast Merlin into a deep sleep".

But the woman shook her head. "Wizards have their ways", she said seriously. "You should know; your uncle was one".

"You mean silly old Hocus. He could scarcely raise a hex. He was always flying into trees and turning people into frogs when he didn't mean to". He laughed at the old memories.

"But this babe is different", she said thoughtfully. "For one thing, he does not cry. For another, he has the bluest eyes I've ever seen".

"Come here, kitchy-koo", said the woman with instinctive maternal affection, and even before she had finished speaking, the babe was nestling between her ample breasts.

The man looked on while the infant deliberately closed one eye in an exaggerated wink. "The little lecher", he hissed, through clenched teeth.

"Gurgle - gurgle goo", said the infant loudly and the woman gave him a kiss. The man saw the other eye of the infant close.

"This is monstrous", he squeaked, and ran towards the infant with upraised fist.

The woman looked at him as if he had gone mad. "Stop this nonsense at once. Can't you see the little darling's hungry? Get him something to eat".

The man departed with ill - concealed bad grace but when he returned his hands were full of little chocolates for the infant to eat.

"Gimme", said the baby appreciatively, throwing him an approving look.

"It speaks", yelped the man in alarm.

"Of course, I speak", said the prodigy. "You never allowed me to".

"Holy Hell", said the man. "By all that's sacred, are you really Merlin?"

"Yes", said the infant, in a surprisingly grown up voice. "I am Merlin".

"But why the disguise?" asked the man.

"It's a long story," said the infant evasively.

"Do tell", implored the woman.

"We've got all the time in the universe", said the man.

"Vivienne came to learn magic from me, as you probably already know", began the infant. This was the stuff legends were made of and the two listeners nodded. "Unfortunately for me", he said, " she learnt too well".

"No, it isn't really what you think", added he imp. "Not a case of a doting wizard enamoured of a young enchantress".

"Vivienne was my first love", he continued, and had the grace to blush. The woman squeezed his hand in sympathy. "Also my last, I must confess".

"Vivienne was as old as I," he continued. "I first saw her at the beginning of time and the stars shone brighter when she smiled. I knew even then that she was the only woman I would ever love."

"Was she very beautiful?" asked the woman.

"I don't know", said the child simply. "She filled my world and that was good enough for me".

"And then?" pursued the woman.

"Vivienne never cared for me", said the child in a hollow voice. "What need did she have for wisdom, for ancient lore? She was a child of nature, wild and free, a harlot from the day she was born. She was naturally promiscuous, an eternal wanderer but she meant no harm. No man could be her harbour. She is still out there, looking for something she will never find".

"Herself?" offered the woman perceptively, and the child nodded gravely.

"She came to me one day and told me she wished to marry. I knew she intended some treachery because Vivienne was not the kind a man could hold. But I yielded and gave her the spell to bewitch.

The man she was after was a noble prince and Vivienne could not have hoped for a better suitor. But I killed the man, as surely as if I had run a knife through him.

She had drained him of his soul in less than a year and left him a pathetic ruin.

Don't judge her, Vivienne was no ordinary woman. She was a creature of the woods, born to mate and move on as often as the seasons changed. She had no heart".

The woman shuddered at the desolation in the child's voice.

"One day, she asked me for the secret of eternal sleep. I could read her thoughts and guessed at once why she wanted it. The only voice of conscience that she heard was mine because she had no conscience herself and it irked her. She wished to still it forever and be free. I laughed aloud and she knew I knew.

But it did not prevent her from pursuing the secret, and one day I discovered her foraging deeply among my most ancient scrolls.

Vivienne was not that kind of woman to blush when she was discovered. Instead, she offered me her body in some kind of expiation."

"And?" asked the man softly.

The baby blew a bubble at him. "Naughty, naughty", he said, and the man had to laugh.

"I knew she would not rest until she had destroyed me, and anyway my work in this world was done. So I decided to humour her."

"But what of Vivienne?" asked the woman?

"Ah, what of Vivienne?" echoed the baby.

"Vivienne lives in every female spirit of the forest, Vivienne lives in every woman who hates man. Vivienne will always live as long as there are men and women. Vivienne is the very stuff of life. I did worship at the altar but the candles were lit by other hands". His voice faltered.

The woman looked a question at the babe and he answered. "I gave her the spell all right but it was not the spell of eternal sleep, it would only last three millennia and I would be reborn. I went deep, deep, deep into the womb of time and have only now returned."

The infant hesitated. "What Vivienne did not know was that the spell had the power to rebound on its user. Vivienne too, went into a deep, deep sleep soon after".

The woman planted an impetuous kiss on the infant's cheek. "Thank you, kind lady", said the babe and, with a swift kick to the husband's bottom, he vanished. "Good-bye, arsehole", came floating on the wind to the couple's ears and they smiled at each other.

Far, far away, in a distant universe, a man's face, handsome and forlorn, looked up piteously at a woman, a woman beautiful beyond belief. A feral smile formed itself on the woman's lips and the man gave a wail of despair. Merlin had not spoken the whole truth. Vivienne too, had awoken when he had......

In their love-making that night was a passion the couple had not known for millennia. Meanwhile, in an ancient castle a lonely wizard shivered and a single lamp flickered defiantly in the cold wind.

*****

16.

A Way With Bores

The stranger came in, out of an awful night. His eyes were as mean as the weather, cold and forbidding. His fur coat was streaked white with snow and the hat on his head as soggy as a sponge.

He shook himself like a great bear, spraying huge droplets of water all over the room, and then headed for the corner table, where he settled himself down heavily. He asked for a whisky and the bar tender promptly provided it. The bartender watched with growing concern as several more whiskies followed. It could mean trouble if Old Mother Liquor spanked the stranger too hard. He looked towards his bouncer, who nodded, alert in case of trouble.

But the man showed no signs of being drunk. The alcohol must have warmed him, though, because he unbuttoned his coat.

It was nearing closing time and the bartender announced last orders. "Bring me three", said the stranger in a voice, which brooked no argument. The bartender hesitated but obliged. Business was business and the man had not misbehaved yet. He glanced at the bouncer again, satisfied he was ready for trouble.

The bartender had an end-of-evening ritual of having a quiet beer with his last customer. But something about the stranger troubled him, as though he knew him from somewhere, some other time and place, far in the past. But the memory remained maddeningly elusive.

"Care for a drink?" asked the stranger casually, as if he knew of the bartender's last-drink habit. "Don't mind if I do", said the bartender. "You too", said the man, glancing at the bouncer. The bouncer looked at the bartender for permission and received a smiling thumbs-up.

They settled down in comfortable silence, broken only by tinkling ice. At length the stranger looked up and asked, "Care for a real drink?"

His companions looked puzzled. "Isn't this whisky good enough for you?" asked the bartender, a trifle truculently.

"No offence meant, friend", said the stranger, raising his hand. "But I know a formula that could teach a mule how to kick. Care to try it?"

"Why not?" said the bartender, his professional curiosity aroused.

The stranger made his way to the bar and began mixing various drinks in different measures. He returned with three tall glasses, the liquid in them a dark orange tinged with green.

"What is it?" But the stranger only smiled at the bartender as they sipped their drinks. "Great", said the bouncer, and the bartender nodded in agreement.

The stranger mixed them another drink and then another. It was close to 3 a.m. when the bartender got to his feet. "It's time to pack up", he said unsteadily.

"Have another", said the stranger, good naturedly.

"No, we really must close", the bartender was adamant. "Rules are rules".

"Well, if you insist", said the stranger. "But don't you want to know the recipe?"

"Yes, of course," replied the bartender.

"Then you must have one last drink with me," insisted the stranger.

"Okay, you win stranger. Maybe we can bend the rules just this once", laughed the bartender.

The stranger got up, went to the bar and returned with three fresh glasses. This time, along with the glasses, he placed an old photograph on the table. As the bartender looked at it, he started in surprise.

"This is a photograph of my wedding. Now I remember you, that's you in the background. You were sweet on her, but as I recall, there was no ill will".

"There wasn't. There still isn't", said the stranger. "So let's drink to that" and the three men drained their glasses. "Now here goes, I keep my promises. Take a peg of rum, and add a peg of whisky and add some lemon juice and Worcester sauce. Stir for 30 seconds. Add white wine with Ajinomoto then orange juice and coriander leaves. But the last drink of the day is the one with the secret ingredient, the one no one ever lives to learn about". He paused. "And this will really slay you.... To the last drink, I always add a little white powder". He turned to his glassy eyed companions. "But you aren't listening are you? Anyway, just for the record, you add a bit of arsenic."

He sighed, closing the staring eyes of the two men. He proceeded to take out a sharp bowie knife and carve his initials on their forearms It was a way he had with dead bores.

*****

17.

Reunion

They had all flown in for the reunion, from different parts of the country, and some had even come from abroad where they now lived. There were bear hugs and cool kisses and the air was heavy with uttered profanities. Thirty years is a long time, too long to conceal the ravages of time. The vain had dyed or peroxided their hair; others had patted down the remnants of receding hairlines and breezed in unselfconsciously. Cries of "Oh my God, is that you?" and wisecrack replies on the lines of "No, it's my maiden aunt", echoed round the room.

The remains of the Class of ¾ had gathered there out of a sense of tradition, curiosity, good fellowship and a dozen other reasons.

"This is a bonus – there's so much more of each of us to see", was another wisecrack. Most of them felt like survivors from a shipwreck.

Someone must have organised the get-together because suddenly he stepped up to the rostrum.

"Welcome old cocks and hens," he began until shouts of "Down Fatty" nearly drowned him out.

He continued undaunted. "This is an evening that none of us will ever forget". He paused to glance slyly at the liquor cabinet, raising a laugh. "But before we do, I would like to offer a small prayer for those of our friends who are no longer with us". The announcement was sobering and the list depressingly long which drew cries of "Christ", and "What a shame", from the audience. Mercifully, it came to an end but succeeded in driving everyone to the bottle.

"Here's to death", said an old classmate seated next to me. "The sooner the better", I replied blandly to cries of "Hear, Hear", from those around us. We drained our glasses and refills arrived at once.

The liquor flowed freely and as the years slipped away so did the masks and disguises The presidents and vice-presidents of corporations and advisors to governments in more than a few countries, went back thirty years in time.

Groups naturally aligned themselves according to old friendships. Stories were swapped; news updated, deaths tut-tutted over, divorces applauded. Lapels had tags with designations printed on them so there was no need to ask who did what. Very organised, I thought. You could smell the power in that room, naked and brutal, almost as if it had a definite aroma.

I looked with curiosity around the room. I noticed that there were very few women; surely there had been more than those present here. As if on cue, I saw her just as she entered the room. I gave in to an immature desire to ignore her and turned away. It was as if I had seen her the first time and I reacted with the one-upmanship of the very young. Slipping into old habits is easy, I reflected ruefully.

I did not know if she had seen me but she veered away from where I was standing. From the corner of my eye I saw her making her way through the crowd. Reviving old loyalties, I presumed.

A hearty slap on the back upset my drink all over the table. I looked round to see a dear, old friend grinning evilly from ear to ear.

"Gobbo the Goblin", I said rudely. "Park your arse". He obeyed with alacrity and proceeded to poke me in the stomach. "What's happened to all the muscle?" he taunted.

I didn't take the bait. I looked down my nose at him with dignity. "Act your bloody age, screwball", I said mildly.

"He'd turn into triceratops if he did that", said a feminine voice behind me "And stop bloody well ignoring me. It's thirty years since anyone did that".

I looked up resignedly. "And so the three of us meet again".

"In sunshine, thunder or in rain" they added in unison and we cackled together like midnight hags.

Quite naturally Gobbo took over leadership of our little group and became what I can best describe as the convening witch. The other members of his coven were relieved and slipped into their familiar roles. I had reached the stage where any more alcohol would turn me from my usual passive self to a truculent aggressor and I cautiously put my glass down.

My love of a hundred years ago glanced at me approvingly, giving me the kind of look no woman should give a red-blooded man. But then, who said I had any red blood left in me?

Gobbo called the meeting to order. "This is no accident", he said solemnly. "This was preordained". We nodded solemnly in agreement.

"Do you remember?" he began and then burst into song. "Do you remember an inn, Miranda? Do you remember an inn?" Miranda, for that is what we shall now call her, nodded. I felt a chill descend on me, for we were moving dangerously near to truths.

I remembered that bloody inn only too well. We had gone there, the three of us, young, with the future ahead of us and very little experience behind us. It was the opposite of the present, I reflected morbidly. What had we to look forward to? I must have sighed aloud, for Miranda looked at me oddly. "What's with him?" she asked.

"Gone bloody maudlin", said Gobbo, who always had the answers.

"Poor boy", said Miranda, kissing me full - bloodedly.

"Hey, less of the pornography", chided Gobbo, refereeing this little byplay of the sexes.

I got myself another drink. I was damned if I was going to be cautious tonight. Where had caution led me? I wondered bitterly.

"Getting back to the inn", said Gobbo, tenaciously pursuing the subject. "You do remember, don't you?" he asked pointedly.

"Yes, we remember", the woman said, her eyes had an avid gleam.

"Power," I said.

"Yes, power", said Gobbo with relish. "How I like the sound of that word."

"Power," said Miranda, looking as hungry for it as she always had.

"Did you find it?" I asked him.

"Did I find it?" he echoed. "Of course, I found it." He bent his lapel towards me and I laughed right into his face. That nettled him and he grabbed hold of my lapel and peered at it. " What the hell have you done with your life? Squandered it in bloody quatrains, I'll be bound".

"Don't squabble like spoiled brats. What's wrong with quatrains?" Miranda intervened. "They're a darned sight more intellectual than couplets". This feeble attempt at humour restored a sense of balance.

"Yes, I found power", said Gobbo, who was now a kingmaker of sorts. "I found power such as you cannot imagine. I am a satisfied man". He looked up proudly and behind his hooded eyelids I saw a broken marriage, a crippled daughter and a liver steadily deteriorating. I saw the loneliness that screamed out from behind his shallow facade. But I could not help him.

"Power", said the woman. "I found it, too. I always knew I would". I wondered if the beds slept in, the compromises with life had been worthwhile.

It had been prophetic, that day at the inn when they had both opted for power and I had shied away from their vision of the future.

Since then I had often wondered if it was lack of courage or drive that had prevented me from being like them. I saw them now, deities of their chosen worlds and I suddenly wished I was far away.

"And did you find power, too?" Gobbo asked me facetiously, fairly gone on his drink.

"I found you two", I replied simply.

That seemed to amuse Gobbo. "Power by proxy". He chuckled.

"I suppose", I said quietly.

The woman got up suddenly. "Have to sleep. Flight to catch early tomorrow morning". She gave me a brief kiss and Gobbo a wave.

Gobbo suddenly came out of his stupor. "Me, too. I'm leaving. But I'm damned if I'm going to kiss you",he said, as he planted a wet kiss on my cheek. "Beddy-bye time", he sang and stumbled out of the hall.

I helped myself to a last drink in an attempt to rid myself of the heaviness that had settled on me. The meeting had left me disturbed. It was terrible being forced to admit one was a cipher.

I got up and went out onto the lawn. I strode

past the weeping woman and the man who lay sprawled out under the stars, his lapel turned up aggressively, but I did not stop. I was ready to return to my world and I had a flight to catch

As I sat musing in my plane seat, an epitaph popped into my head, fully formed: "Time and flights wait for no man / Power and pelf are a shit can". Quatrains were well beyond me at the moment, but I felt hugely pleased at my effort.

Reality was a whole sleep away.

*****

18.

Virgin Come Lately

We had made love everywhere, any which way, any which how, there was little we had not done together. The chemistry was spectacular from the instant we had set eyes on each other. And, somehow, morals and such minor considerations had become irrelevant. Yes, there was a husband, but he seemed self-sufficient and uninterested in the female half of their partnership. Perhaps, I told myself, he had even encouraged my attentions, was ,maybe, even aware of how things stood between us.. After all it had been fifteen years since it had begun – the affair, I mean.

As time passes, deception becomes easier and the ploys and stratagems to meet become routine. Explanations are tedious and take the spice out of a relationship; so none were asked for or offered by either of us.

The years had been kind to her and it was always with pleasure that I looked at her body. I had not fared so well but she did not seem to mind.

I was quite content, the affair continued and grew into years and I never felt the need for commitment, even marriage. The relationship demanded nothing of either of us and lasted through long separations. We would always meet again afterwards as if we had never been apart. There did not seem to be any reason for the relationship to end.

After one particularly long period of being apart, – she had gone abroad with her husband for a year – we met again at her house. Alone with her, I looked forward to a pleasurable night of lovemaking. The evening began like many others we had shared, with drinks and inconsequential conversation as we slipped back into the pattern of our relationship. It was as if she had never been away. We were always careful not to delve too deeply into each other's personal lives and this, I felt, was the foundation on which our long lasting liaison thrived. It was difficult, but stimulating.

Neither of us wanted to be responsible for the other realising that if you begin to feel too deeply you end up doing all the wrong things

That night, the music was good, the scotch heady, and the conversation lively. I took her in my arms as I had a hundred times before and the preludes to lovemaking began.

Lost in the pleasure of being with her again, it took some time to get through to me that she was unresponsive. Was it something I had said?

"Is something wrong?" I asked. She shook

her head but I knew something was worrying her. She drew away from me and then got up to refill her glass. She sat down again on the chair next to mine.

"I'm sorry", she said simply.

Unsure of what had just happened, I didn't know how to react. "What's the matter?" I asked again. She took a deep breath and then, as though her courage had failed, she stayed silent.

I drew closer to her and in an effort to reawaken her desire, kissed her on the lips, my hands roving over her body. She was rigid and I felt like a necrophiliac.

I looked at her and I think defeat must have shown on my face because she made an attempt to explain. "It's nothing to do with you. It's my husband".

Nothing could have surprised me more, A minor player assuming a major part in the play at the penultimate stage.

"Your husband?" I croaked. "But there's been nothing between you for decades".

"We've managed to work things out", she told me, but she seemed nervous. "You didn't believe we could, did you?"

It was like a kick in the stomach, sudden and unexpected. "I'm very happy for both of you," I said, but could not resist adding, "If it has actually happened".

She felt obliged to defend herself in the face of my patent disbelief. "I won't say the chemistry is wonderful, but yes, we do make love now. And I'm really too old for deceptions. I don't have the nerve any more. And besides – I know it's late in the day – I do feel a little cheap".

I gaped at her. I had been dismissed after fifteen years with this incredible explanation. Something didn't add up in this glib scenario.

I was suddenly conscious of my hand trapped between her thighs. "Congratulations", I said dryly. "And now, please, may I have my hand back?"

She laughed and quickly released my hand.

Where do I go from here? I asked myself. I had gone fifteen years without looking at another woman and now I was alone with no family to fall back on, no wife or children to share my declining years.

What had I done with my life? Jezebel had no right to turn into an untouchable virgin. It was so bloody unfair. She had plunged back into security, leaving me out in the cold.

It was the enormity of her transformation into the faithful wife which had knocked me base over apex. This coyness seemed out of character with the image I had of her. It is always difficult to make a dignified exit in these situations but I began to feel stupid continuing a conversation that had lost all meaning. I waved goodbye, and this final farewell felt no different from all our temporary ones of the past.

I stood outside her flat, feeling soiled, relegated to the role of home wrecker, an interloper between husband and wife. I was amused at her virtuous stance because I could have sworn that she didn't have a moral bone in her body. But the new persona she had created was unassailable.

My unease that something was not right was given confirmation by her expression which had not been honest. Her fairy tale story about rapprochement with her husband didn't ring true. I had also seen another expression in her face. An expression of impatience or was it anticipation? Of what? It troubled me.

As I stood there perplexed, lost in my reverie, the solution to my confusion walked past me. I saw the door to her house open and close behind the young hunk and shortly afterwards the lights in the bedroom went out.

But I was already walking away, my stomach

tucked in to its limit. I promised myself I would return – when I was fifteen years younger.

*****

19.

Will You, Won't You?

It was a magical night; the kind of night anything could happen because there was an air of unreality. The gathering was as strange as you would find anywhere, their weird masks heightening the atmosphere of disorientation. The invitation to the party had been quite specific; a mask was a must for all guests.

Jabberwocks rubbed shoulders with Napoleons, while Batwomen hobnobbed with Cinderellas. A hundred masked figures cavorted grotesquely on the dance-floor. Pandemonium reigned; no one was quite sure of what lay ahead and no one cared. The music was loud and the excited shrieks of the crowd added to the din.

Strange friendships were struck up that night and I was no exception to this. I had danced with a Rapunzel, a Sappho and my latest partner was a Puss-in-Boots. I had come as the scarecrow from Oz, a simple disguise for me because I possessed a large assortment of torn clothes that I simply did not have the heart to throw away.

"Oh you look positively scrumptious", said Puss-in-Boots. "How deliciously dirty", I simpered foolishly. Clever women always unnerved me.

"Good puss, sweet puss", I responded, offering her a glass of wine. Her cat's face regarded me seriously. "I really mustn't", she said. "After all, I am your hostess. If you'll excuse me... I'll be back in a moment." She swirled away gracefully.

When she returned, she had changed her mask. It was still a cat but the expression had grown sombre, almost sinister, I felt.

"Let's get everyone drunk", she said. "Wouldn't that be just perfect?"

I nodded my head dubiously. She seemed to take that for assent for she purloined a tray of drinks from a passing waiter and proceeded to offer it around.

We became friendlier and friendlier as the night moved on to its riotous finale. When it was time to leave, she offered me her hand and said, "Come". I followed without question.

She took me to an apartment overlooking the sea. It was unexpectedly seedy, in contrast to her stylish manner and appearance. When we entered the drawing room, she shrugged as if in apology, "It's not much", she said. "But it's home."

I did not know what to say but my heart went out to this lovely apparition who lived in this place that was not worthy of her but who remained ethereally unaffected.

"I love this place", she said unexpectedly. "I really love it here".

I did not know if she meant it but she seemed serious. She put on some music and then she was in my arms and we were dancing.

Her breath was sweet and I was swept away by her. I saw her face, serene and happy.

In the morning we woke up in each other's arms.

"Thank you for a very lovely evening", she said. "I would like to give you a gift, a book to read. You must promise me you will only read it once you are home. It would be a bore if you looked at it now."

I eventually left in a haze of alcohol and love, not quite steady on my feet. I knew I would return soon and the thought made me deliriously happy.

The very next day I stood in front of the apartment again and rang the bell. A stranger opened the door.

He did not know anyone that fitted the description of my Puss-in-Boots. He had just moved in that day so perhaps it was the previous tenant. I rudely stepped passed him into the room but it bore no resemblance to the apartment I had been in the night before. The landlord was no help either. He found his tenants through managing agents and rarely met them in person. No, he did not know the woman who had lived there.

Puzzled, I returned home. The only connection to her now was the gift she had given me and I idly picked up the book. The title was an odd one, *Creative Poisoners,* and I wondered why she had given it to me. Disturbed, I read on.

My unease grew as I read the factual accounts of notorious murderers who poisoned their victims. When I turned to the final story in the book I felt my blood congeal. Above the caption "Notorious woman poisoner who throws masked balls to trap her victims" smiled the face of my Puss-in-Boots.

I learned that she fed her victims either fast or slow acting poisons, depending on her whim.

I ran for the newspapers and found the headline I hoped would not be there. "The Maniacs Masked Ball - 20 guests poisoned. Search on for host".

Had I, like a few other lucky guests, been spared? Or was I reserved for her expertise in slow poisoning? Was toying with the mouse part of the cat's pleasure? Shocked and unsteady, I made my way to the local library hoping to research poisons and their antidotes.

The art of poisoning is complex, I read, for some poisons can lie dormant for a decade.

Every day now, I watch my face for signs that all is not well. I will do this for the rest of my life and, wherever she is, I know she is laughing at me. Or perhaps she took pity on me for the momentary pleasure I gave and took me off her list. As I live between dread and hope, I sometimes think she must have hated me the most.

Every month, I receive another copy of the book. My efforts to trace the sender have proved fruitless..

Last week, along with the book, I received a small packet of white powder. Written on the packet were two words. "Eat me", just like in Alice.

I can sense her enjoying the horror she has made of my life, knowing that she has sent me an invitation I will one day accept. God bless her evil heart.

*****